SKATE MONKEY

For the students of
Waiheke Primary School, Aotearoa

First published 2017 by
Bloomsbury Education, an imprint of Bloomsbury Publishing Plc
50 Bedford Square, London, WC1B 3DP

www.bloomsbury.com

Bloomsbury is a registered trademark of Bloomsbury Publishing Plc

A CIP catalogue for this book is available from the British Library

ISBN: 978-1-4729-3339-3

Printed in China by Leo Paper Products

1 3 5 7 9 10 8 6 4 2

recommended by
www.catchup.org

Catch Up is a charity which aims to address the problem of underachievement that
has its roots in literacy and numeracy difficulties.

Story inspired by *Monkey* by
Wu Ch' Êng-Ên, c1500–1582

PAUL MASON

SKATE MONKEY

THE CURSED VILLAGE

Illustrated by
Robin Boyden

SKATE MONKEY

Monkey and his friends, Zu and Sandy, lived in the Jade Emperor's Cloud Palace. But they played all sorts of tricks on people, so, as a punishment, the Jade Emperor sent them down to Earth.

They can only return to the Cloud Palace if they prove that they can use their magical powers for good...

CONTENTS

Chapter One

The train pulled into the station. The brakes on the train screeched.

"Weston. Last stop. Everyone off!" said the driver over the speaker.

Sandy looked out at the grim station. "Hey, wait a second, this isn't where we wanted to go," she said.

"Zu, did you make us get on the wrong train?" Monkey growled.

"Oops," said Zu looking at the timetable in his hands. "My mistake."

The train doors opened. Monkey, Zu and Sandy stepped off the train. It was cold. They zipped up their jackets. Monkey pulled a hoodie over his scruffy hair. They dropped their skateboards onto the platform.

They walked out of the station. They could see the town of Weston at the bottom of the hill. The streets were empty and dark. Then they heard a church bell ring.

"This seems a really spooky place," said Sandy. She shivered and pulled down her hat.

"Now what do we do?" asked Zu.

"Let's ask him," said Monkey.

An old man in a long, dark coat stood just outside the station. He carried a black bag in his hand.

"What time is the next train back to the city?" asked Monkey.

"Ha!" laughed the old man. "There isn't a train until tomorrow morning. You will have to stay the night in Weston."

"You're joking!" said Sandy.

"There is a hotel on the High Street. You could stay there," said the old man. He picked up his bag. "Enjoy your stay," he said with a strange smile on his face. Then he rushed off down the hill and vanished into the shadows.

"Great,' said Monkey. "Now we are stuck in the middle of nowhere."

"Hey, maybe this could be a test, Monkey," said Sandy. "The Jade Emperor did say if we proved ourselves we could go back home."

"You reckon?" said Monkey.

"First, let's find this hotel. I need something to eat," said Zu. He jumped on his skateboard.

Chapter Two

The friends skated into the town. They didn't see anyone. All the houses were dark, with their curtains closed.

They found the hotel. Monkey read the sign. It said *"Welcome Hotel."* The hotel looked closed. Sandy tried to open the door but it was locked. Monkey banged on it with his fist.

The door opened a crack. The landlady stuck her face out. "What do you want?" she asked.

"We need a room for the night," said Monkey.

The landlady looked them up and down. She looked worried. "You had better come in," she said. She opened the door.

"Not very welcoming, is it?" Monkey said to Sandy.

Inside the hotel, a fire burned in the fireplace. The landlady showed Monkey, Zu and Sandy to the table next to the fire.

"Where are all the other guests?" asked Sandy, looking around.

"No one comes to Weston any more," the landlady grumbled. She went off to the kitchen. She came back with three plates of food.

Monkey, Zu and Sandy started eating their dinner. Suddenly, from the street came a horrible noise. It sounded like an animal crying out.

Zu jumped to his feet. "What is that?" he shouted.

Chapter Three

The three friends rushed to the window. They opened the curtains.

Monsters. An army of monsters staggered down the street.

Their faces were pale, and their eyes glowed red. Blood dripped from their mouths. Their long claws shone in the light of the moon.

"Zombies!" Sandy gasped.

"The town is full of them," said Zu.

Now, they saw a man running down the street. The man ran for his life. The monsters ran after him. They got closer and closer.

"We need to save him!" yelled Monkey.

The landlady opened the door. "Quickly! Come inside!" she shouted.

The man ran towards the hotel. The zombies closed in on all sides like a net. They snatched at his legs. They clawed at his arms. The man stumbled and fell to the ground. The zombies swarmed over him. The man cried out, and then went silent.

The landlady quickly shut and locked the door. "There is nothing we can do for him now," she said.

Chapter Four

"Just what is going on?" asked Monkey. The landlady sat down by the fire. Her hands shook.

"Weston is under a curse," she said. "The town is ruled by Jiangshi. Creatures that are half zombie, half vampire."

"Where did they suddenly come from?" asked Zu.

"Nobody knows. They only come out at night to hunt for blood," said the landlady.

"That is why the church bell rings. The bell is a warning."

"The old man at the train station didn't say anything about that," thought Monkey.

"If someone gets caught by the Jiangshi, they turn into one of them," explained the landlady. "Then they have to follow the master. The master controls the town."

"Who is the master?" asked Sandy.

"We don't know," said the landlady. "But if we can catch the master, we can stop the curse."

"But why hasn't anyone in the town sent for help?" asked Zu.

"We've tried and tried, but no one believes us," said the landlady. "The police just laughed when we told them."

"Maybe we can help you," said Monkey.

Chapter Five

The next day, the town was quiet. There was no sign of the Jiangshi. The three friends decided to skate around the town and take a look.

In the town square was a market with some stalls. There were only a few people shopping.

"In the old days, this market would have been full of people," said a woman selling fruit and veg. She waved at one of the shoppers. "Good morning, Dr Blade."

"Good morning," said Dr Blade. Monkey saw it was the strange old man from the station. The old man came over to say hello. "Oh, it's my friends from the train. I didn't think we would meet again," he said with a smile.

"We're still here," said Monkey.

"No thanks to all the Jiangshi," said Sandy.

"So you know about our terrible secret," said Dr Blade. He sighed. "It is very sad. Our town is cursed."

"We want to help beat the Jiangshi," said Monkey.

"We want to find the Jiangshi master," said Sandy.

"Why don't you come to my house and have dinner? You can stay the night," said Dr Blade. "I can tell you everything I know about the Jiangshi."

"That sounds good," said Monkey.

"Excellent," said Dr Blade. "I live next to the church. Come to my house just before it gets dark."

"We'll be there," said Sandy.

Dr Blade waved goodbye. Monkey watched the doctor as he walked away. "There's something about him I don't trust," thought Monkey.

Chapter Six

That evening, Monkey, Zu and Sandy went to the doctor's house. The sun was setting. Next to the doctor's house was the church graveyard.

There were gravestones, and dark statues. In the middle of the graveyard was a large, stone building. The doors of the building were locked shut.

"Creepy," said Sandy looking at the building.

Monkey knocked on the doctor's door. There was the sound of footsteps. The door opened.

"Good evening," said the doctor. "Come in."

The three friends went inside. Dr Blade showed them to the dining table.

"Please sit," he said. "Wait here. I won't be long. Dinner is almost ready."

"What are we having for dinner?" asked Zu.

"It's a surprise," said the doctor with an odd smile. He went to the kitchen.

The friends waited for him to come back.

"Dr Blade has been gone for a while," said Sandy.

"What is he doing?" said Monkey.

The friends went into the kitchen. There was no food cooking on the stove. There was no sign of the doctor. The kitchen was empty. The door at the back of the house was wide open. The friends could see it was dark outside.

"The doctor left the door open!" said Zu.

"The Jiangshi could come in!" gasped Sandy.

"Look," said Monkey. They could see someone with a torch over by the graveyard. It was Dr Blade.

"The doctor is up to something," said Zu.

"Come on, let's take a look," said Monkey.

Chapter Seven

The friends jumped over the fence. They hid
behind a gravestone. They watched Dr Blade.
The doctor had a torch in one hand.

In his other hand he had some keys. His black bag was on the ground by his feet. He was in a hurry. He was trying to open the door to the creepy building. His key was stuck.

Then the doctor heard them. He turned around and shone his torch. "Who is there?" said the doctor.

Monkey, Zu and Sandy stood up. "What are you doing?" asked Monkey.

"I was checking that this burial chamber was properly locked," said the doctor. "There's been so much trouble lately."

"But you weren't locking those doors," said Sandy. "You were trying to open them."

"I guess you caught me," said Dr Blade with a smile. "But I'm afraid you're too late!"

He pulled the chamber doors open.

A horrible screaming came from inside.

Suddenly, the Jiangshi came out of the dark. Their mouths dripped with blood. They grasped with their claws.

"The secret hiding place of the Jiangshi!" said Zu.

"Get them!" ordered Dr Blade.

The Jiangshi attacked.

Chapter Eight

Monkey reached into his jacket. He pulled out a pen. "Full charge," he said. The pen flashed and crackled as it changed shape.

The pen grew and grew. Soon it was the size of a baseball bat. Monkey spun it around in his hand.

Sandy got out her smartphone. "Upgrade!" she cried. The smartphone changed shape. It became a huge metal pole. Sandy twirled it round her head like a windmill.

Zu reached into his pocket. He pulled out a fork. "Supersize!" he called. The fork turned bright red. It glowed like fire. The fork became bigger and bigger.

It turned into a huge, metal rake. Zu slammed his rake onto the ground. The ground shook. Some of the Jiangshi tripped and fell.

"Come on!" said Monkey.

The three friends rushed forwards. Monkey
swung his bat left and right. Two beasts
crashed to the ground. Sandy did a flying kick.
Zu charged with his rake.

But the Jiangshi kept coming. They scratched and grabbed with their long claws. They tried to bite with their fangs.

"You'll never win!" laughed Dr Blade.

"He's right," said Sandy.

"We can't fight them all," gasped Zu. "There are too many."

"We can if we have help," said Monkey. He pulled three hairs out of his head. He blew on the hairs.

He said the words of a magic spell. There was a flash of light. Suddenly, there were three more Monkeys in the graveyard. Each Monkey held a fighting stick.

"That's better!" said the Monkeys all together.

"No!" shouted Dr Blade.

Chapter Nine

The Monkeys charged at the Jiangshi. Sandy hit out with her pole. Zu shoved with his rake. The friends pushed the zombies back.

One by one, the Jiangshi stumbled back into the chamber. They cried and moaned. Monkey reached for the chamber doors. He pushed and pushed. At last, he slammed the door shut.

Sandy and Zu grabbed the old doctor.

"Game over," said Monkey. He said some magic words and the other Monkeys disappeared.

"Now, take away the curse, Dr Blade," said Sandy.

"You win," gasped the doctor. "Pass me my bag."

Zu brought the doctor's black bag.

"No tricks," said Monkey. He raised his bat.

The doctor reached inside the bag. He brought out a glass bottle. "This is the potion that turns people into Jiangshi. I used it to take over the town," said Dr Blade.

"Here, take it." Dr Blade held out the potion to Monkey.

Monkey reached out to take the bottle. Suddenly, Dr Blade pulled back his hand and threw the bottle down on the path. The bottle smashed into pieces. A cloud of green smoke filled the air. "You'll never catch me!" screamed Dr Blade. Then he vanished.

"No!" said Zu. "He got away."

"Listen," said Monkey. He pointed at the chamber.

The wailing inside the chamber had stopped. Sandy opened the chamber doors. Inside were some very scared people. They were not zombies anymore. They were back to normal. "It's over now," said Sandy. "Time to go home."

Chapter Ten

The next day, the streets of Weston were a happy place. The town square was full of people. Monkey, Sandy and Zu skated back to the train station. Everyone stopped to thank them.

The friends waited on the platform for their train. "It felt good saving the town," said Monkey.

"Now do you think the Jade Emperor might call us back home?" asked Sandy.

"You have to admit, we were pretty strong and brave and wise," said Zu.

"We'll have to wait and see," said Monkey. "But something tells me our challenges aren't over yet."

Bonus Bits!

Test your knowledge of Skate Monkey: The Cursed Village. Turn to the back for the answers (no peeking along the way!).

1. When can Monkey, Zu and Sandy return to the Cloud Palace?

a)   When they have defeated a bad person

b)   When they have proved they have used their magical powers for good

c)   When they have apologised to the Jade Emperor

2. Whose fault was it that they were on the wrong train?

a)   Zu

b)   Sandy

c)   Jade Emperor

3. Who banged on the hotel doors with their fists?

a)   Zu

b)   Monkey

c)   The old man

4. What made Monkey, Zu and Sandy look out of the window and see the monsters?

a)   a sound like a ghost

b)   a sound like a car horn

c)   a sound like an animal crying out

5. Why were not many people at the market?

a)   There were not enough stalls

b)   There is a market in a different town

c)   They are scared of the curse

6. Who do they need to find to break the curse?

a)   The Jade Emperor

b)   The Jiangshi Master

c)   A zombie

7. Where was the secret hiding place of the Jiangshi?

a)   Burial chamber in the graveyard

b)   Dr Blade's house

c)   The market in Weston

8. What did Monkey's magic spell do?

a)   Kill Dr Blade

b)   Conjure more Monkeys

c)   Attack the Jiangshi

9. What happened to Dr Blade at the end of the story?

a)   He took over Weston

b)   He was killed

c)   He vanished

Who owns which Superpower?

Can you match up the character with their object, magic words and magic objects? Turn to the back for the answers (no peeking!).

CHARACTERS:

Monkey

Zu

Sandy

OBJECTS:

fork

pen

phone

MAGIC WORDS:

"Upgrade"

"Full charge"

"Supersize"

MAGIC OBJECTS:

pen the size of a baseball bat

huge metal pole

huge metal rake

The Author

Paul Mason is the author of this story. Here are a few interesting pieces of information about him:

- He LOVES writing and writes all the time, but he admits that he is rather slow at texting!

- He likes writing books for children and making them fun to read!

- He lives on an island.

- He has a cat called Kipling

- He also claims to live with a Flemish Giant called Rex?!

What next?

If you were a character in the story, what object would you choose to have? What would your magic words be, and what would the object turn into? Write a short story using the characters from this story and yourself where you need to use the thing you have chosen.

Answers to Quiz

1b 2a 3b 4c 5c 6b 7a 8b 9c

Answers to Superpower:

Monkey – pen – "full charge" – pen the size of a baseball bat

Sandy – phone – "upgrade" – huge metal pole

Zu – fork – "supersize" – huge metal rake

Look out for...

SKATE MONKEY
Fear Mountain

Chapter Three

The sun was setting. Monkey, Zu and Sandy rode their skateboards to the funfair. They came to a stop. They kicked up their boards.

Rory met them at the front gate. "Thanks for coming," he said. Rory let them in. He shut the gate and locked it.

"Wow, this place is huge," said Zu.

There was a tall roller coaster high above them. Just down the path was a haunted house. Nearby, a giant pirate ship rocked up and down. At the far end of the funfair, there was a dark, rocky, mountain with a log flume ride. A waterfall poured down the mountain into a lake.

"Where do we look first?" asked Sandy.

"Let's split up," said Monkey. "Sandy and I will start with the roller coaster."

"And Rory and I will start with the bumper cars," said Zu. "And maybe stop at the food stall," he grinned.

"Be careful," said Monkey. "Whatever beast is leaving those giant paw prints is out there somewhere."

"Thanks for reminding me," said Zu.

"Let's go," said Monkey. He dropped his board to the ground and raced off.

"A terrible cry came from inside the funfair: the cry of a beast..."

Giant footprints, strange noises, wrecked food stands... something is going on at the funfair and Skate Monkey and his friends need to find out what!

9781472933430